This Little Tiger book belongs to:

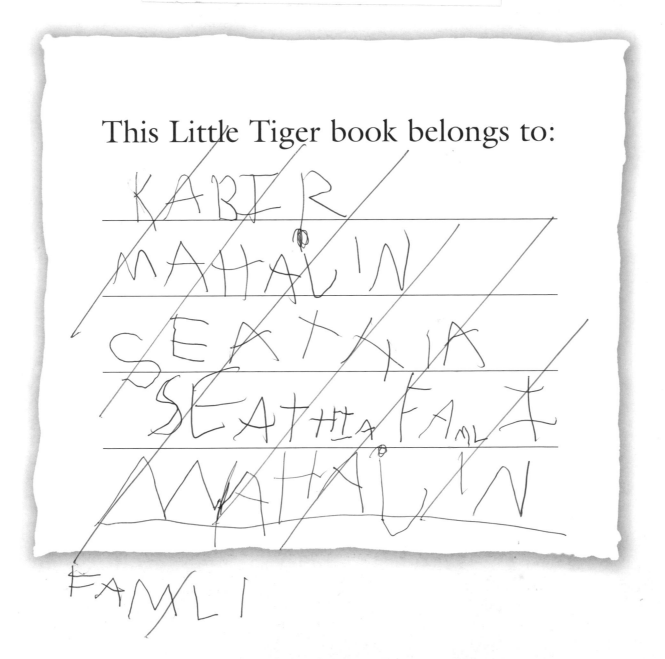

KABIR

MAHALIN

SEATHA

SEATHA FAML

MAHALIN

FAMLI

Don't be so nosy, Posy!

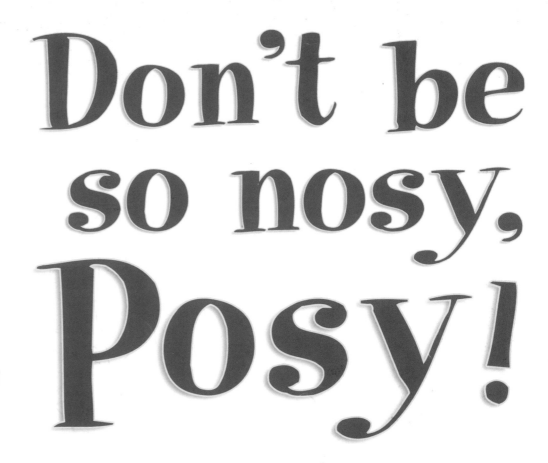

By Nicola Grant

Illustrated by Tim Warnes

LITTLE TIGER PRESS

Posy the piglet didn't mean to be nosy. She was just very interested in knowing things.

"Who wakes *you* up each morning?" she asked Ronny Rooster.

"Does it hurt to lay an egg?" she said to Hetty Hen.

"Questions, questions!" the animals sighed. "Don't be so nosy, Posy!"

But Posy wanted to learn things. Even if it did sometimes land her in trouble!

One morning, Posy was playing
'don't tread on the daisies' with
Cowslip Cow. As they skipped under
an oak tree they heard a strange noise.
  "I wonder what that is?" said Posy,
peering inside a hollow in the oak to look.
  "Oooh! Don't do that, Posy!"
cried Cowslip, but it was too late . . .

Posy raced off quickly, chased
by some very angry bees!
  "Oh, Posy, you do look funny!"
Cowslip laughed. "You've got
honey all over your nosy nose!"

The next day, Posy was playing in the farmyard when she spotted the farmer's tractor nearby.

"I wonder what *this* does?" she said, pressing a big red button.

BEEEEEEP! blasted the horn. Posy tumbled out in a heap!

"Who's playing with my tractor?" yelled the farmer, running up.

"It's Nosy Posy!" clucked Hetty Hen. "And she's woken me from my nap!"

"Sorry!" Posy squealed. "I'll try to play more quietly!"

But Posy couldn't stay quiet for long!

"Do you feel chilly without your warm woolly fleece?" she asked Sally Sheep on shearing day.

"Tell me, do you keep noses in your nose-bag?" she laughed at Harry Horse.

"How silly!" mumbled Harry. "One day you'll learn not to be so nosy, Posy!"

But Posy didn't think so!

Then, one sunny day, Posy and Dilly and Dally Duck were playing piggybacks. "Ooooooooooh!" came a strange noise from somewhere across the field. "Sshh!" whispered Posy. "What was that?" "Oooooooooooooooooooooooooooooooooh!" came the ghostly cry again, even louder!

"Let's find out what it is!" Posy said excitedly.

"Don't be nosy, Posy!" quacked Dilly and Dally.
"Whatever it is, it sounds scary!"

"Scaredy ducks!" Posy laughed back. "Come on!"

Posy ran across the field, with Dilly and Dally
tiptoeing behind.

A large, dark shape loomed through the trees.
They crept closer . . . and closer . . . until they saw . . .

Cowslip Cow with her head stuck in
a fence!

"Oh, Posy, I'm so glad to see you!"
Cowslip cried. "I squeezed through
here to reach some tasty clover, and
now I'm trapped. It's terrible! Please
help me!"

Posy and the ducks pulled and
pushed, and pushed and pulled—but
Cowslip's head wouldn't budge!

"I'll never get out!" howled Cowslip.
"My head will drop off! Help me, Posy!"

Mooo

"The farmer will rescue you!" said Posy. So
they all cried out at the tops of their voices.
   "HELP! HELP! HELP!"
   But the farmer was with Harry Horse
in the stable, too far away to hear.
   "I knew it!" wailed Cowslip. "I'm stuck
here forever!" And a big tear fell from
her eye with a plop!
   Then, out of the corner of her eye,
Posy spotted something that was sure to
bring the farmer running . . .

Posy pressed the tractor's horn.

BEEEEEEEEEEEEEEEEEEEEEEP!

Up the field raced the farmer!
And behind him came all the other
animals, clucking and squawking,
neighing and bleating, to see what
was happening.

"Oh dear me!" cried the farmer.
"OK, everyone. You all push, and
Harry and I will pull. After three.

One . . .

TWO . . .

THREE!"

"Heave!" gasped the animals.
"Squeeze!" shouted the farmer.
"Ooooh!" gulped Cowslip.
Suddenly there was a very
loud OOMPH!

Everybody cheered. Cowslip was free!
"Hoorah for Nosy Posy!" she mooed
happily. "If it wasn't for her, I could
have been stuck there forever!"
"It was nothing!" said Posy proudly.

"We'll never complain about your questions again!" the animals told Posy. "In fact, you can ask us anything you want!"

"OK! What's this for, Dilly?" Posy asked, looking at a large blue hosepipe lying nearby.

To Jason
~ *NG*

For Tim, good boy, well done!
~ *TW*

LITTLE TIGER PRESS
An imprint of Magi Publications
1 The Coda Centre, 189 Munster Road, London SW6 6AW, UK
www.littletigerpress.com

First published in Great Britain 2004 by Little Tiger Press, London
This edition published 2008

Printed in China

2 4 6 8 10 9 7 5 3

fantastic reads from Little Tiger Press

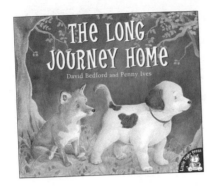

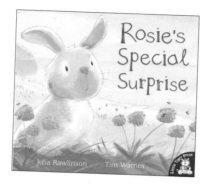

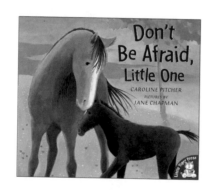

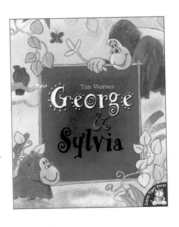

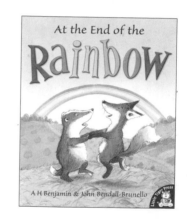

for information regarding any of the above titles
or for our catalogue, please contact us:
Little Tiger Press, 1 The Coda Centre,
189 Munster Road, London SW6 6AW, UK
Tel: +44 (0)20 7385 6333 Fax: +44 (0)20 7385 7333
E-mail: info@littletiger.co.uk
www.littletigerpress.com

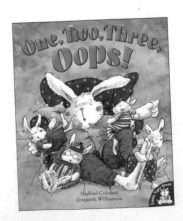